For Tomene
With huge thanks
to B, J, R & L

In loving memory of Andrew.
Thank you for making this happen.

Inspiring | Educating | Creating | Entertaining

Brimming with creative inspiration, how-to projects, and useful information to enrich your everyday life, Quarto Knows is a favourite destination for those pursuing their interests and passions. Visit our site and dig deeper with our books into your area of interest: Quarto Creates, Quarto Cooks, Quarto Homes, Quarto Lives, Quarto Drives, Quarto Explores, Quarto Gifts, or Quarto Kids.

Text © 2018 The estate of Andrew Gibbs. Illustrations © 2018 Zosienka.
First published in the UK in 2018 by Frances Lincoln Children's Books
First published in the USA in 2019 by Frances Lincoln Children's Books,
an imprint of The Quarto Group.
The Old Brewery, 6 Blundell Street, London N7 9BH, United Kingdom.
T (0)20 7700 6700 F (0)20 7700 8066 www.QuartoKnows.com
The right of Zosienka to be identified as the illustrator and Andrew Gibbs to be identified
as the author of this work has been asserted by them in accordance with the
Copyright, Designs and Patents Act, 1988 (United Kingdom).
A catalogue record for this book is available from the British Library.
ISBN 978-1-78603-591-2
The illustrations were created using gouache paints.
Set in Baskerville
Published by Jenny Broom and Rachel Williams
Designed by Zoë Tucker
Edited by Katie Cotton and Kate Davies
Production by Jenny Cundill and Kate O'Riordan
Manufactured in Dongguan, China TL112018
1 3 5 7 9 8 6 4 2

FSC
www.fsc.org

MIX
Paper from
responsible sources
FSC® C104723

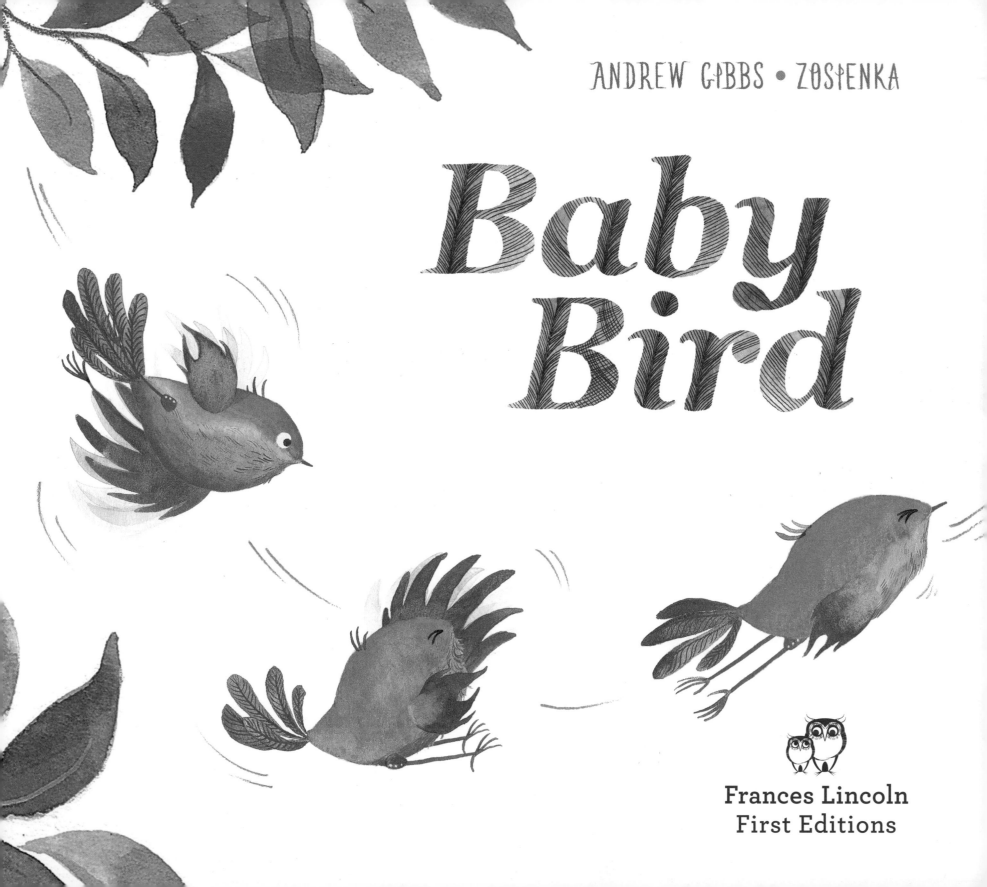

ANDREW GIBBS • ZOSIENKA

Baby Bird

Frances Lincoln
First Editions

Baby Bird was *different* from the
other hatchlings. One of Baby's wings
was twisted and shrunken and not
at all like the other one.

Baby's brothers and sisters all had two matching
wings, and as time passed they grew bigger and stronger.

Soon the time came for the
hatchlings to leave the nest.
Baby watched the others
flap and fly away.

"Birds are born to fly,"
thought Baby. "I suppose
it's now or never . . ."

So Baby took a big run up and yelled,
"Wait for me!"

Baby flapped . . .

grrr

and flapped . . .

and . . .

THWOMP

Baby watched the other hatchlings
swooping and laughing as
they played together.

"It's all so easy for them," Baby thought.
But close by was a little bridge
and a soft patch of grass, and
it gave Baby an idea . . .

"That's the perfect spot to learn to fly!"

Baby practiced flying
all morning.

Really, it was more like falling,
but Baby was determined.
"I'm not giving up!"

Suddenly Baby heard
a rustling in the bushes.
Something dark was moving
beneath the bridge . . .

In a flash, a shape burst from the
shadows and landed beak to beak with Baby.

"Aaaah!" Baby screamed. "A monster!"

"Aaaah!
Where?
Where?!"

"Oh, *me*?" said the monster. "I'm not a monster—
I'm Cooter! Nice to meet you! I've been
watching you jumping up and down over
and over again. Whaddya doing?"

"I'm not *jumping*," said Baby.
"I'm *flying*. I just haven't got
the hang of it yet."

Cooter spotted Baby's
little wing and gasped.
"Holy baloney!
What happened?"

"Nothing!" snapped Baby.
"Leave me alone!"

"Sorry," said Cooter. "I didn't mean
to make fun. But you might need a buddy
to help get you flying. Whaddya say?"

Baby thought about it for a while
and said, "That would be great."

Baby and Cooter
practiced flying
all afternoon.

They tried the
King Swing . . .

the Spring Launcher . . .

. . . and plain old jumping and flapping.
But nothing worked.

As the shadows grew long,
Baby decided to take a break.

"Never mind!" Cooter said. 'I sure am
having fun with you, anyway.
You wanna go swimming now?'

"I'm not *having fun!*" Baby exploded.

"And I don't want to swim! I'm not a fish. I'm a bird,
and I'm learning to fly, like all birds should,
so that I can join the others in the sky."

Cooter looked sadly at Baby and said,
"I don't think you'll *ever* be able to fly with that little wing."
Baby thought: "Cooter's right. I am a baby bird.
I have a broken wing, and I'll *never* fly."

Baby flopped down on the bridge, feeling *very* tired . . .

and *very* sad
and *very* heavy . . .

But then . . .

Baby flapped . . .

and flapped . . .

"What am I going to do?"
cried Baby, safe on Cooter's back.
"I'm a bird. Birds are born to fly, but I can't."

"Hey," said Cooter. "I'm a bird and I'm a *terrible* flier."

"Really?" Baby gasped.

"Yep!" said Cooter. "It's never bothered me."

"I know what'll cheer you up," said Cooter. "Some good old-fashioned Coot Scooting. I've always done it alone, but I sure think you'd love it."

Baby frowned. "What the heck is *Coot Scooting*?"
"I'll show ya!" said Cooter, spreading his wings.
"Hold on!"

Coot Scooting was frightening at first,
but soon, as the world whizzed by,
Baby forgot to be scared and started laughing.

"You know something?" said Cooter, laughing too.
"What?" yelled Baby, into the wind.

"You don't need
strong wings to fly."